HOW MANY SLEEPS 'til Christmas?

by Mark Sperring ❄ Illustrated by Sébastien Braun

tiger tales

One winter morning, before the sun had even woken,
Little Pip climbed out of bed, padded across the floor,
and "PSSST!" gave Daddy Grizzle a gentle nudge . . . .

Daddy Grizzle yawned and stretched
the way he did every morning,
then plumped his pillow and . . .

ZZZZZzzzz

fell right back to sleep.

"WAKE UP!" said Little Pip.
"I think it's Christmas Day!"

Daddy Grizzle opened one VERY sleepy eye.
"No," he mumbled.
"It isn't Christmas Day yet . . . .

"In fact, there are **four** sleeps
'til Christmas—
FOUR whole sleeps
to wait."

Little Pip gave a disappointed sigh.

"But don't worry," said Daddy Grizzle.
"After all, we **still** have PLENTY
of things to keep us busy."

First, they needed to find a tree . . . .

So out they went, Daddy Grizzle and Little Pip,
and searched until they found the perfect tree,
waiting quietly in the frosty woods.

And that night, they decorated the tree with all kinds of ornaments and lights, then cuddled up in the comfiest of chairs.

"**FOUR** whole sleeps 'til Christmas,"
Daddy Grizzle reminded Little Pip.

"Okay, Daddy . . ." murmured Little Pip.
"One . . .

two . . .

three . . . ."

But the next morning, a certain someone seemed
to have forgotten something very important . . . .

"PSSST!" said Little Pip.
"WAKE UP! I think it's
Christmas Day!"

Daddy Grizzle climbed out of bed
with a BIG bear GROAN.

"No," said Daddy Grizzle,
    "it isn't Christmas Day yet.
There are three sleeps 'til Christmas—
    THREE whole sleeps to wait."

"Three . . ." sighed
Little Pip. "Three . . . ."

But perhaps that was just as well.
    After all, they hadn't sent a single
        Christmas card.

After Daddy Grizzle and Little Pip had written their cards, out they went for a br

Then, when they got ho

alk, only stopping to shout, "SPECIAL DELIVERY!" at the top of their voices.

y—YiPpEe!—found some Christmas cards of their own.

And by the time Little Pip was tucked in bed,
not only had Daddy Grizzle displayed the cards . . .

"how Many Sleeps?"

but he had also explained
something that still
needed explaining.

three sleeps
'til Christmas

The next morning, Little Pip was just as confused as ever.

"PSSST!" said Little Pip. "WAKE UP!
I think it's Christmas Day!"

Daddy Grizzle rubbed his sleepy eyes.
"No," he yawned. "No, no, no,
not now! Not yet! First we
have some presents to wrap!"

So they both sat down, and (without looking over their shoulders once) wrapped two "No Peeking" presents to be opened first thing on Christmas morning.

That night, after they had placed their presents
under the tree, Little Pip watched
the Christmas lights
shimmer,
SHINE
and twinkle
before climbing
into bed.

To Little Pip,
Love from
Daddy GRIZZLE
xxx x x x x x

To DADDY
GRIZZLE
Love from
Little Pip xxx

"Try to remember," said Daddy Grizzle,
    hoping to make things clear,
"there are two more sleeps
    'til Christmas . . .

TWO whole sleeps to wait."

But of course, Little Pip did NOT remember . . . .
"PSSST!" said Little Pip early the next morning. "Today I'm SURE it's Christmas Day!"

Daddy Grizzle scratched his head.

"No," he said, peering out into the snow-covered woods.
"First, we need to make some **special friends.**"

They made two snowmen—one **BIG**, one small—
and both with **BIG**, happy smiles.

Later that night, Little Pip asked, "HOW MANY SLEEPS 'til Christmas now, Daddy?"

"Well . . ." said Daddy Grizzle with a thoughtful look, "we found a tree and delivered our cards . . . .

"We wrapped our presents and EVEN made two new friends . . . .

"Now, there's nothing else to do.
So it's only **one** sleep 'til Christmas—
only **ONE** sleep to go."

"One!" smiled Little Pip. "**Just ONE!**"

And **EVEN** Daddy Grizzle felt
a shiver of excitement.

The next morning, EARLIER THAN EVER, a certain someone woke up and realiz very special day was FINALLY here . . . .

"PSSSST!"

And when Little Pip opened his tired eyes,
there stood Daddy Grizzle, wide awake and beaming.
   "WAKE UP, WAKE UP, Little Pip!" cried Daddy Grizzle.
"It's YOU-KNOW-WHAT!"

Little Pip gasped and Daddy Grizzle let out a **HUGE** cheer
that rattled the windows and woke up the entire forest . . .

"HooRay! HooRay! It's REALLY Christma

For Nel and Al (her Daddy Grizzle) — M. S.

For Leonie with love — S. B.

tiger tales
5 River Road, Suite 128, Wilton, CT 06897
Published in the United States 2014
Originally published in Great Britain 2013
by Puffin Books
Text copyright © 2013 Mark Sperring
Illustrations copyright © 2013 Sébastien Braun
ISBN-13: 978-1-58925-160-1
ISBN-10: 1-58925-160-1
Printed in China
SCP0214
10 9 8 7 6 5 4 3 2 1

For more insight and activities, visit us at www.tigertalesbooks.com